Adhuri Prem Kahaniya

Adhuri Prem Kahaniya

"The weakness of a man is the strength of a woman"

Santosh Avvannavar

www.power-publishers.com

Power Publishers
www.Power-Publishers.com
Swabhumi Residency,
P-12 Motijheel Avenue,
Block 2, 1st floor,
Kolkata 700074.

Printed From

Ray Dot Com
College Street,
Kolkata 700073, India

ISBN: 978-93-83271-39-9

First Published: September 2013

Price: ₹ 150/-

Cover Design
Utsav Lall

This book is dedicated to: -

The Almighty God,
Parents,
Raghunath Babu Are,
Sameer Mirji,
Sujeeth Kumar,
Ruchita Kumar,
P V Ramana
& Dr. Meena R Chandawarkar

Dhanyavad (Thank You)

I would like to thank the Almighty God for giving me ability to pen stories. I thank my parents for their unconditional love and support. I express gratitude to my best friends Raghunath Babu, Sameer Mirji, Vasudha Mirji and Amresha M for being there during all the time of trials. I would also extend my gratitude to the mentors Meena R Chandawarkar, P V Ramana, N K Narasimhan; Suchita Khanna, Avinash Himanshu (Facebook motivators); Ashwin Bellur, Sujeeth Kumar and Ruchita Kumar (Emotional support).

I would also like to thank all the twelve people that agreed to share their stories to make this book a reality. I also thank Amrita Foundation for HRD (www.amritafoundation.wordpress.com) to allow me to pen all my thoughts since May 2012. I would like to thank Utsav Lall, Vidhya Shree V and Ashar Neyaz for giving color to the book through artwork and liners to the book. If someone is missed to thank this could be only accidental not intentional.

Last but not the least to all my dear students!

Why it's Adhuri?

The thought of writing this book existed since childhood and it has propelled by influence of mainly Bollywood romantic movies such as DDLJ, QSQT, JTHJ, MPK and others. I still remember asking a question to my mother, is it all about at the age of 20 was you were to get married to an unknown man, move to your in-law place and that's your life? Did you ever fall in love with daddy? I liked her reply to it, I always wanted to fall in love with your daddy but I was busy managing people and home. As time passed you were born and I got busy taking care of you. I only know that we are happy.

I grew with this institution of love. Not to generalize here, the meaning of love has taken its own shape with fast paced life. There are many couples that are depressed about their love lives. That is why I believe in the Facebook relationship status "It's complicated" exists. The whole intention of this book is to make those people realize that there are many people like you who have fallen in love and have learnt to move on. It's completely natural. You can either make it or break it. But what is it that breaks a relation? This book will help you to know those hearts stamping moments that you can prevent happening to you. Each chapter is a story of one person, one might feel that the story ends abruptly or conclusions are not drawn appropriately. This is done intentionally for the readers to synthesize the climax.

I recall a dialogue said by a famous Hindi film actor Shahrukh Khan to Rani Mukherjee (dressed as bride groom) both seated on a bench in Kabhi Alvida Kehanna Movie "Mohabbat Ke Zamaane Guzar Gaye Janaab, Ab Chote Mote Pyar Se Hi Kaam Chala Lijiye Aap" (Sir, the age of love is over ... you should work it out with a small affair). I would like to mention another movie liner to complete the reason behind 'Adhuri' title for this book from Jab Tak Hai Jaan movie "Har Ishq Ka Ek Waqt Hota Hai, Who Waqt Hamara Nahi Tha, Iska Matlab Ye Nahi Ki Who Ishq Nahi Tha" (Every love has its own time, that time was not ours, but that doesn't mean that the love itself wasn't ours).

Happy Reading!

With Love,

Santosh Avvannavar

Love is patient, love is kind. It does not envy, it does not boast, it is not proud. It is not rude, it is not self-seeking, it is not easily angered, it keeps no record of wrongs.

-1st Corinthians 13: 4 – 13 (NIV)

Aaj Hamari Zindagi Kitni Badal Chuki Hai,
Jisme Tu Kahan Hai Aur Main Kahan Hun,
Tere Jaane Baad Ye Zindagi Tanha Si Ho Chuki Hai,
Jisme Tu Kahin Hai Aur Main Wahin Hun…

- Ashar Neyaz

Contents

Prem Kahaani: Pehla Bhag

Meri Pehli - Thanda Paani

Meri Doosari - Sutra Dhar

Meri Teesri - Dosti, Dushamni Aur Ladki

Meri Chauthi - Dil Toh Baccha Hai

Meri Paachvi - 1 2 Ka 5 'Doosari = Paachvi'

Meri Chati - Akhari Sarkar

Meri Pehli - Thanda Paani

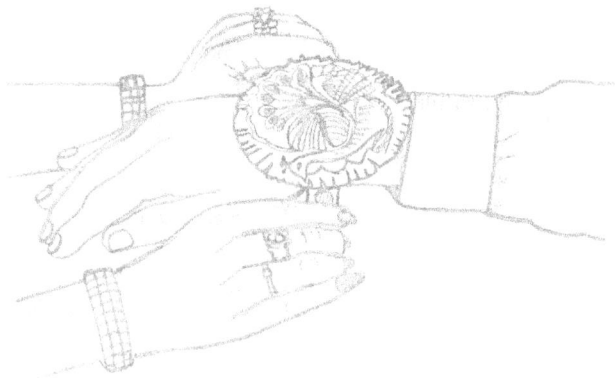

Oxford dictionary say *Infatuation* is an intense but short-lived passion or admiration for someone or something. I don't completely agree to this meaning, as I haven't forgotten this, as it's still an intense. I haven't stopped admiring it as well and no wonder you are reading it as well. I was just 13-year-old studying 8th standard with ample influence of romantic movies, as most common love stories are through medium such as 'common friend and marriages.' Thanks to social network now, that has fueled more opportunities. I met Shraddha through a common friend at school. During 9th standard annual fest, we had a competition in which we were supposed to pick a coin from ice-cold water. Luckily perhaps then (not sure about that luck now) we bumped into each other for this competition. She asked me, 'Kya hai humare beech mein?'(What is between us?). I was so innocent that, I replied "cold water." She giggled and some giggles are never short-lived. During this fest, I dedicated a song to her 'I love you sanam..' Not sure why I did this stupid act? This created a strong ripple, as rumors spread about us across the campus. She started showing a lot of restlessness and a day I never dreamt of - she walked to me and said, 'I want to tie you a Rakhee.' Oh God!

Why does such things exist? A ribbon tied, a relationship get turned from 'B2B' - *Boy Friend to Brother*. I had to become 'Saaiya' to 'Bhaiya,' unexplainable moment though! Meri Pehli ... not sure what to name this relationship - girl friend or sister? I will leave this to the readers to name it.

Meri Doosari - Sutra Dhar

Love life has many 'Sutra Dhar,' suffocation of being in a big fat family and my prayer to move away from home was heard by God. I received a call from Montosh Uncle (First Sutra Dhar) from Bangalore in 2007 to see if I am keen to study in Bangalore. I can't express this joyous moment; I packed my luggage and moved to Bangalore next day. Thanks to Mrs. Suzy (Second Sutra Dhar) for helping me to take up admission at Clarence High School, Bangalore. Most of the students were Christians (I know that, I am being stereotyped) and was trying to see if someone from similar cultural background to mingle. The third Sutra Dhar 'Common Subject - Computers' is very important one to take this story forward, I thank the school management for keeping some subjects common to see if uncommon things can happen. I met, Anamika Ghosh and Anamika Jain, luckily doosari is doosari. Perhaps she fell for me in first instance and I received first 'Kabootra' message through Keertna (Fifth Sutra Dhar). I forgot to mention Fourth Sutra Dhar, it's a common scene in many Bollywood movies 'Baarish' thanks to 'Indra' the rain God. I had parked my bicycle expecting for the rain to slow down, but the rain God had different plans. She came rushing on her vehicle and stood in front of me. We stood so close by; Mahesh Bhat (Bollywood Film Director) saheb would be inspired to make 'Aashiqui 3.'

Perhaps it was second *'Infatuation'* - next day in the school she wanted to have an ice-cream with me, I didn't get her pulse of this indication. I asked her to go and have it. She said a word that still touches me 'Dumbo Ice-cream.' We went to 'Flavors' ice-cream hoping for a colorful flavor life ahead. This dream was short-lived, as she asked the cashier to return money paid by me. She said we are just friends. Oh God! It's quite difficult (never possible) to understand which flavor a girl is made up of.

The Wheeler Road was Sixth Sutra Dhar for seven months, I rode my air pumped bicycle and she rode her two-wheeler petrol filled vehicle. We went together on the same road all these seven months and love was in the air. I don't remember writing any letter to parents but wrote a love letter to her. She was not ready for this relationship, she wasn't sure if this going to work out. This sounded strange! Really strange! A typical question she asked me, 'What is future of our relationship?' I felt; let's live in present at least. All of us are so worried of future and miss out on present.

Time (Seventh Sutra Dhar) is the best healer; things looked cementing and shaping themselves. She came to my place and it was my first kiss to a girl; was in the process of loosing virginity.

The Eighth Sutra Dhar was just another guy in the story; on a fine day a guy slapped me infront of others in the school premises. I couldn't bear this insult; phones rang asking friends for help. As sun set there were typical hit-out session and she witnessed it all. Perhaps climax was nearing! I told her that

'Koi pyaar kara toh mujshe kare, mai jaise hua waise kare, koi mujhe badal kar pyaar kare, toh woh pyaar nahi, saudha kare, aur sahiba, pyaar mein sauda nahi hota...'

'One should love me, the way I am ... if someone tries to change me in love, then its not love but a compromise ... and darling, one doesn't compromise in love ... right?'

These Mohabbatein (Bollywood movie) liners didn't impress her much. I decided to depart from her by returning most of the letters, cards and gifts, burnt her photos, started smoking and spoke about it all the time to friends and continue to talk. Till date both of us are not sure, why we broke up? Bus ho gaya…

Meri Teesri - Dosti, Dushamni Aur Ladki

I learnt to move on and took coaching at 'Brilliant Tutorials' during 2008 for IIT-JEE admissions. It was a rainy day; I was seated in a class and heard someone's voice at the door. 'May I get in?' Some voice touch heart, her wet clothes touched me more than that. 'Alma' meri teesri girl friend! We bumped into each other at times in the class, as she sat in front of me. Hi, Hello gestures turned to phone calls and Yahoo! Chat. One day she asked me over the phone, 'We are more than friends right?' As still innocent I said, 'Yes we are Best friends'. Thanks to the pagan tradition for introducing Birthday Celebration. I wanted to be the first person to wish her at midnight. On her birthday I carried two roses, I gave one rose saying - 'This one for the beautiful woman' and the other rose I gave proposing her. She walked away without saying anything with carrying a smile on her face. It reminded me a of saying, 'Ladki Hassi Tho Passi.' I am not sure how many times this liner worked. We were blissful, days passed.

I received a phone call from her, 'Hi, I am alone at home - Do you like to come over?' Is there any fool that would reject such an offer? In no moment I crashed my bicycle onto her house, then there were hugs and kisses. The hand was about to move into other corners, 'Ding Dong - Bell Rang.' It was her parents at the door, panicking situation. I ran with my shoes and hide in her room under the bed. In sometime I suggested her to send parents away for a while. I was finding all the theories of escapism. I hid below the bed as her mother knocked the door. She sat on the same bed, looked like mountain fell on a mole. I hid under the bed for 3 hours before some respite came to rescue. The bladders were running full; tension prevailed and all looked like 'Chakravyuh' battle. I never knew this theory of escapism until that day.

Some stories have villain and India Bollywood movies have them all the time. Sudarshan, a playboy cum villain cum friend stole Alma's mobile number and started dating with her. He was a man of idea 'F&F.' I got to know about their dating through another best friend Prasoon. My mind didn't agree to Prasoon and we had a quarrel on this issue. Within some days Alma decided to depart, as I questioned the relationship between her and Sudarshan. I knew, I had lost her and it was Holi festival. I never wanted to loose my best friend Parsoon, knocked his door to wish him colorful holi. Door opened with a newer twist, Alma was with him. My future looked dark in mist of colorful holi festival. Meri Doosari gave me cigar; Teesri gave me sea of depression.

Meri Chauthi - Dil Toh Baccha Hai

With deep depression I finally landed with an engineering seat in 2009. I didn't have more faith in love and trust in people. Fortunately heart (Dil Toh Baccha Hai) doesn't seem to understand all these. Some common events bring people together and it was personality development program during the first semester. Not sure if any personality developed but was sure that the love was reborn, it was Jhanavi. She was beautiful and a playful girl. We met often over lunch and dinner as most of people do while they are dating. One night she called me and proposed 'I Love You.' These words (perhaps only Love) have made and ruined the world. After a moment of proposing, she disconnected the call. Often history repeats, this incident reminded me of Anamika. I dialed Jhanavi and asked her, 'Did you try to find about my feelings?' 'What is the future of our relationship?' I don't know about future, lets be together atleast for four years. I felt for a while, am I a toy for four years to use?

As days passed, not only I, my friends also felt that, 'I deserve a better girl friend.' Compatibility was the issue, as she had a short-term goal of four-year boy friend against long-term goal as life partner. I called it off this time. Meri Doosari gave me cigar, Teesri gave sea of depression and Chauti gave me Madira (Alcohol). I became a complete new era Devdas with duwa duwa; Anurag Kashyap would be inspired to make U-D!

Meri Paachvi - 1 2 Ka 5 'Doosari = Paachvi'

If I look back and do a comparative analysis on my girl friends - I bet on Anamika. She was matured and best among all the girl friends till someone else came into my life. I was looking for a shoulder to lean and felt she could be the right one. I tried hard to get back to her, but inspite of trying to tie knots of love but things never passed further.

Meri Chati - Akhari Sarkar

Everyone need to start things afresh however the past. I was recommended to attend Art of Living course named as Yes Plus by my uncle. I was in second year of engineering 2010, like me many people were there to seek healing to the painful soul. I found a new friend (Anubhav) and we used to hang out most of time during this course. Anubhav wanted to meet a friend and asked me to join him. I never knew life would take a new turn, an oily haired and shabbily dressed Vanshika (Meri Sarkar). Neither I had any more attraction for a girl nor faith in love (doesn't mean something else!) until a phone call changed this view. She received a phone call from her grandpa. A phone call changed the law of repulsion to attraction. Her Punjabi (I being stereotype) words just caught my attention. Introduction through Anubhav didn't expect that the world would change for us. SMS followed phone calls followed by meetings to dating. I started playing pranks with her, called her once from my dad's mobile number. Madam, calling from Axis Bank - would you be interested in a personal loan? She said, No thanks! I rang the phone again and said, Madam its personal love (Pyaar ka) loan from the bank of my love.

Experience gives many skills to test the present. I met her at Garuda Mall, her traditional attire made me feel she is the one my family would accept. A possession grew towards her and she was leaving away for few days, I couldn't hold that moment. She was about to leave in an auto rickshaw, Vanshika suno (listen), she turned - I hug her. This was perhaps the first time she hug a guy.

Days passed, I was waiting for a sign to propose her. We were sitting at Sankey Tank, like any other lovers we had our own love names like Shonu, Jaanu and others. She pointed towards a rainbow in the sky and I felt the sign to express my love. I bent on knees and proposed her 'I love you.' She was numb and shocked with happiness! She didn't reply to this proposal. I kept asking her the reply, but she kept smiling. This smile kills! We left the place in an auto and saw a beep on phone 'I Love You Too.' The mind still want to hear those three words, although not sure why? and What is the power of these three words? In her low voice she finally said those three words - 'I Love You.' This was the first time we held our hands. We are together since 2 year 7 months hoping from Adhuri to Poori Prem Kaahani.

I know that there are few more hurdles of difference in sub caste that people at both hometowns still think about it. I am like Raj from DDLJ (Bollywood movie) waiting to marry her with parents' permission. I am hoping to see her father say, 'Ja Vanshika..Ja Vanshika..Tumhe ise aacha ladka koi nahi milage..Ja apni ziddagi jeela..Ja Vanshika.' Pray to make this a poori prem kahaani!

Prem Kahaani - Doosra Bhag

Pehla Pehla Pyaar - Guys, Guns, Goons Aur Jati

Pehla Doosara Pyaar - Ek SMS - Mard Ka Dard

Doosara Aur Teesara - Pyaar Ka Safar

Pehla Pehla Pyaar - Guys, Guns, Goons Aur Jati

The transition age from teenage to adolescence is like melting ice, with physical and psychological human development. Among all the developments 'Sexual attraction or erotic attractions', neither parents talk about it nor taught at many Indian schools. I moved from a village to a town 'Bidar' in1998 to pursue college degree (XI std). I stayed at (Bade Papa/ Taya) relatives place; the house was located at the crossroad. The other side of the cross road there was a house of 'Mera Pehla Pyaar.' I had a close friend Ramesh; he was in love with her. My heart did sink on knowing we like the same girl. I approached her on behalf of Ramesh (love proposal) and she said in her sweet low voice, 'If your friend (Ramesh) can't say this directly, how will he lead life with me?' 'Himmatwala ko Himmat nahi hai kya?' Unfortunately for him things didn't work, it always remained one side. Perhaps I am sure there are million's of such 'Adhuri Ek Taarf Ki Prem Kahaniya' (Single Side Love Stories). This was a quite mixed reaction to me, one side a friend loosing his love and on other-side her 'availability' gave me hope. On learning that I am also in love with the same girl, Ramesh gave me green signal by saying 'Gaddar (Back Stabber) ...Kaminey (Mean Minded).'

I was liked by most of people in the lane because of my studious nature, handsome, great gully cricketer, and above all owned Yamaha bike. Whenever my bike honked near the cross road, she would come running and peep from her room window or come out of the house. My friend seated on bike said to me often 'Ladki line derahi hai, Bhai.' I did notice from that moment onwards, we started rising in love.

I will give a sample example for the kind of intensity it had - Being in village or town the disadvantage for Premi's (lovers) is that most of members in villages or town are known to each other's. We could think of meeting only in late in the night or early morning, the latter was easier. I used to get up early morning at 3 am, bathe and reach temple before 4 am. I used toilet vent pipes to reach ground floor of house, jumped few walls and ran 2 km to reach the temple. She was wiser than me, she informed her family members saying, 'I have seen a devil in dream and God has asked me to visit for shuddhikaran (purification) of mind.' We sat at distance in temple and spoke for an hour or two. I had to rush home back before the family members open their eyes. I used to go back and sleep in the same bed by changing the previous day clothes.

Phela Goon

As every story has few 'Goons', the 'Phela Goon' was the temple Pujari. Seeing Premi's (lovers) often - pujari informed our parents, a twist! We were beaten black and blue. We were named as

'Shahajan' and 'Mumtaz' for the intensity of love it had stir in the town.

I had to move to NIT Durgapur for higher studies and we were still in touch. We posted and sent letters through a common friend address regularly. Thanks to movie influences, she sent me a letter written with her blood. The amount of unstoppable tears seeing the letter written by blood would have helped to quench one-person thirst. I often visited hometown to meet her in every semester. While I was in third year of engineering, she started receiving marriage proposals. I was helpless and persisted her to hold it for one year so that we could marry after my graduation. My friends and I stopped few proposals by being 'Doosara Goons' on our own. We had all possible quarrels and hit out to stop the various marriage proposals. One fine day a bigger shock was, within next 12 hours she was getting married. Our hearts were broken; my father could sympathize with me. He suggested me to elope with her and never return to town. My father tried hard to unite both families but 'Jati' came in between us. I would term 'Teesera Goon' is Jati; it continues to ruin many prem kahaniya.

Pehla Doosara Pyaar - Ek SMS - Mard Ka Dard

While studying at NIT Durgapur, friends knew about the ongoing love story of 'Shahajan' and 'Mumtaz.' Remya classmate heard my story on regular basis. She fell in love with me, not sure the role I need to assign her in this story. For a while let me call her as 'Mumtaz 2.' In history most of the Emperor's had more than one queen. Looks like every person is in love with someone 'unavailable' person - 'Har kisi ko doosari ki girl or boy friend hi pasand aatha hai' (For everyone others girl friend or boy friend is beautiful or handsome).

My story with Mumtaz ended tragically and in no time 'Mumtaz 2' tried to make me feel that she is there for me. She would speak half broken Hindi, irrespective of her Hindi learning - she taught me Tamil. That's the beauty of a Tamilian!

We were traveling to Kolkata; she was reading SMS from my mobile outbox. There was one message that was stored in outbox, never knew 'Sala ek SMS Mard Ka Dard Banega.' The SMS read like this –

'Geetha ho Meeta ya Smita....yaar tujhe chhaddi pehne ke liye time nahi rehgi'

(Be its Geetha, Meeta or Smita ...you will not have time to wear underwear)

I tried hard to explain her that the SMS was sent by a friend. She kept saying, 'How can you think like this?' How can an SMS call this relationship off? She was fine about my ex-girl friend and all nuisances during that time. I never understood this sensitiveness of a girl; even Shahrukh Khan didn't understand what Katrina Kaif wishes in Jab Tak Hai Jaan. One thing I learnt that day, never be 'available' to anyone easily.

Doosara Aur Teesara - Pyaar Ka Safar

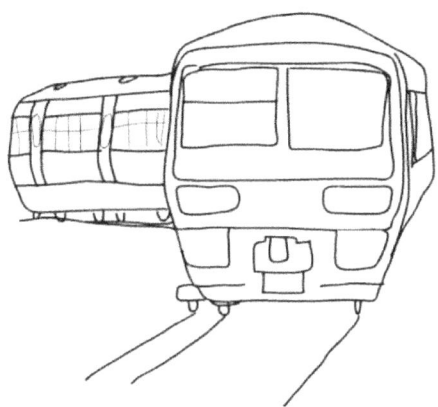

There is nothing new in this story; the only vital in this story is 50 hours time. I boarded train from Yesvantpur (Bangalore) to Howrah and had a head on collision with a beautiful girl in the compartment. She gave a weird look and took her seat. I decided to settle in the same compartment, as there was no reason for other look out. She was traveling with her sister and uncle. In no time I became close to her sister and uncle. We spoke for very long time and it was bedtime. According to wego.com survey on sexual conduct in the skies found that, skies are a potent aphrodisiac for globetrotters. Thanks to curtains for side berths of trains (A.C. Bogies/Coaches) for fueling more to this story and surveys. It was perhaps 23:00 hours; she popped in and woke me. She said in her mesmerizing voice, *'Aapni amar shonge kotha keno korlen na?* (Why you didn't talk to me?). I told her in Hindi that, I only know only one liner in Bengali. She asked, Kya? Smiling I said, *'Ami Tomake Bhalo Bashi.'* Laugh! Laughs!

We spoke from 23:00 hours to next day 04:00 hours, she was about to leave to her bed. I pulled her hand and kissed her on cheek. She ran out of my bed and hide in her bed. Next day she pulled me to lavatory, she brought her face closer and said, 'Tumhade shirt ke pocket mein meda pata hai, meda phone ka intezaar kadna.' Write your phone number on my hand, I couldn't take my eyes from her. We reached Howarh and carrying this wonderful moment I boarded a train to Durgapur. I didn't expect in this short journey of five hour would take destiny one more step further.

'Mitali Banerjee' wore Bengali attire traveling in the same train with her father. I was in my own world; she perhaps thought someone handsome is starring at her. I noticed in sometime and we had 'Aankh mei choli,' I loved her beautiful chocolate eyes. I wish the journey was longer than expected and in no time the station arrived. She asked her father to get down and wait, as she wanted to use the rest room. This was perhaps a hint to me; I pulled her hand and was about to kiss. 'Dekhte parcho na ekhane baba ache?' (Don't you see my father is here?). I just see your beautiful eyes at moment; she kissed on my cheek and ran away. 'Yaar Aankhe Maradegi.' I followed in her bus, sat behind her seat and passed my phone number on a railway ticket from the sideway of the seat. She gave me a flying kiss in return. We spoke often and she learn't that I am Madrassi, everyone in north or east or West India thinks people from south are Madrassi. It took awhile to explain her that I am Kannadiga from Karnataka. As distance was an issue, it never got capitalized. Yeh safar sirf yadgar safar banke rahegaya!

Prem Kahaani - Teesra Bhag

Teri Girl Friend - Meri Girl Friend

Meri Girl Friend - Kisi Aur Ki Girl Friend

Teri Girl Friend - Meri Girl Friend

My roots are from Patna but were brought up in Dhanbad (Jharkhand). As an aspiring candidate I migrated to Bangalore in 2006, beautiful city with much greenery. I was conned by people for an admission; anyway its a different story altogether. I joined for Bachelor of Business Administration course, made friends and through a friend met 'Ranu' girlfriend of a friend. I always thought people fall for someone else's girl friend or spouse only in Shahrukh Khan movies or Karan Johar directions, but it did happen in my life. There were differences between Ranu and her boy friend. Though Kabhi Alvida Naa Kehna (KANK) (Bollywood movie) story didn't convince me earlier, but reality did bite after meeting 'Ranu.' One side she was sad of things not working between (her and boy friend) them and other-side I was waiting for things never to work between them.

Ranu was suffering from heart disease and this suffering brought us near. Sympathy towards her turned to like, like to love in no time. This love was short lived as it had betrayer to take this story with a new twist. I introduced my friends Praveen and Pankaj to Ranu, both started to flirt with her. I was unaware of it and could see changes in her behavior over the period of time. The love turned to hate, hate to hatred as days passed. This story came to end as she started avoiding me and disconnected her mobile number. I will never forget those last moments, 'Hum sirf dost rahenge' (We shall remain only friends), I disagreed to be so. Neither I am a Bollywood actor to sacrifice love and accept as friend anymore nor Facebook status change anytime. We departed!

Meri Girl Friend - Kisi Aur Ki Girl Friend

One side things were not working between us and the other side another story was beginning. I used to pass through girls hostel after the college hours. 'Preeti' one girl among group of girls that I often bumped into on the way, we never missed eye contacts. One fine day she sent a message through my roommate (Ritesh) that she wants to talk with me over the phone. I was puzzled with happiness and spoke with her. She was aware of my past affair with 'Ranu.' We started dating and she often stayed at my place. Until then, I never knew that staying together is known as 'live-in relationship.' There is a saying, 'Ghass dusari taraf hi hari hoti hai' (Grass is greener on the other side), I thought Preeti is all my life. Although this did start with lust and moved onto fall in love but I lately realized that she wanted a guy from a reputed college, rich, smart and accomplished in career. She perhaps was in search of 'customized' boy friend, her particular needs can be adjusted then and there. I was 'standardized' boy friend; you get the same thing all time.

She would read all my SMS but was reluctant to share information from her mobile. I got to know in some days that she dated others as well, while we were in relationship. I could understand apathy of Preity Zinta or Abhishek Bachchan about their partners in Kabhi Alvida Naa Keha (KANK) movie and issue with fidelity. We moved apart saying, 'Alvida' and never thought I would become a great admirer of this movie after this incident. I never understood this liner from KANK but realized it after this incident, 'My life may be incomplete with you, but atleast it will be a life.' Did you understand it?

Prem Kahaani: Chautha Bhag

Saptapadi - Seven Years

Saptapadi - Seven Years

Love stories do happen in small village like 'Aruppukottai' (Near Madurai) with a strong belief of community that, 'Love and marry one person.' Perhaps the ideology is similar to most often repeated dialogue (Hum Sirf Ek Baar Pyaar...) of Shahrukh Khan from Kuch Kuch Hota Hai Bollywood movie. According to science it is said that puberty for boys begin at ages 11-12 and ages 10-11 for girls and complete the puberty by 16-17 ages and 15-16 ages respectively. I may not have understood the process of physical changes, as this was treated as a social taboo (continue to exists now as well) to talk about.

First Vow: DEC 2001, I was a 12th standard student staying at door no 48 and Aishwarya in a diagonally opposite door no 51 studying in primary secondary school; who was pretty to look at. Aishwarya's father Muthuswamy was college friend of my mother Swathi. Muthuswamy was enquiring about me with my mother, wish it were about marriage proposal with Aishu (nick name of Aishwarya). The enquiry was rather about my well-being and change in behavior, I was shocked and contemplated why Muthuswamy enquired such things? It was an awful reminder of 1995 that I had beaten Aishu black and blue while playing. The first vow that I made was never to raise hands on a girl or woman.

Second vow: Inspite knowing that love itself is a social taboo in many villages in India, love for her secretly grew. To show decent behavior and talent, I used to read aloud to catch their family attention. Unfortunately, it never paid any deeds for this effort. I won district level first prize for talent exams (Physics and Chemistry). To boast and convey message about this achievement, found a 'Sutradhar.' Though the plan went as expected but her reaction was, 'What's the big deal?'. I understood that more effort is needed to win her trust and love. A good education and job might change her perspective. I made a second vow that day to get admission in a top college. Having missed medical seat by one single digit went to join engineering at REC Trichy during Aug 2001.

Third vow: May 2002, she attained puberty and this made me insecure that others might eye her. I started to propagate about my feelings to others, as others will maintain distance from her. Beloved brother became a close friend (initially unaware about the hidden agenda) and I used him as Suthradhar for some days. I started calling her brother as 'Machan' (Brother in law) and this word raised doubts. We had a tiff in some days and I expressed to him like Rajnikanth actor, "I can't forget Aishu, I love her and I would marry her. I wont change my mind, its fine to break our friendship, good bye." I made a third vow not have any hidden agenda, be open and straight on your likes.

Fourth vow: June 2002 - DEC 2002, my regularly visits to home irked my father, I sat hours (12 hours or more) at veranda to get her glimpse. My sister and mother got to know about this and they turned out to be supportive. How could this not happen? As my parents was a love marriage and I being their first child in family after their 6 years of their marriage. You see emotions bind people! I made a fourth vow to take support of family first in such situation. The support was to such an extent that they could find minor details such as her birth date, food habits, dress color (green or violet silk salwars), handwriting and others.

Fifth vow: May 2003 - May 2005, Tamil movie such as Alaghi, Mouna Ragam, Guna, Anbe Sivam, Poovay Uoonakagaa and others had influence on many viewers. Such movies have created wonders to many love stories of common people. These movies had positive influence by helping me to differentiate between love, lust and infatuation. One-way influence was positive but it had interesting (rather funny) incidents to quote here, 'I wanted a photograph of her, finally could get a copy of group photograph from her friend. Thanks to advancement of technology that could zoom and get only her face-pic.' I took courage to walk into Aishu house and proposed her; she declined in her low voice. Perhaps not knew how to propose, the liner was 'you love me or not.' No wonder there are so many re-takes for each scene in a movie. I made a fifth vow to work on my liners to perfect before proposing her next time.

Sixth vow: June 2005 - July 2008, having secured a high GATE score and admission at Indian Institute of Science, Bangalore (now spelled as Bengaluru) hoping things would turn positive. As any attempt to contact or meet her failed occasionally, decided to write a letter to her father Muthswamy. I did see a reply from her father saying, lets see after 5 years, as it's too early to comment. Bloody diplomats, in five years I would be a father of two children or more. With lot of perseverance luckily I got to talk to her, this time liner were rehearsed seven times. Unfortunately screwed it up again! I needed more practice and a director to get the liners right. She in turn informed her father and there were lot of miscommunications that began. I made a sixth vow to re-look into my decision of love and life. I waited with anticipation for the stages of caterpillar love to colorful butterfly love for seven years but it always remained as a caterpillar.

Seventh vow: Every love stories have some learning and I have mine here -

1. Dream, imagination and unilateral love are nice to be seen in movies or fairly tale. I am responsible of all the decision and outcome.
2. Each one has own desire and life style to lead. I didn't try to find out about her desire and life concerns. I was there in that story; perhaps she was never there.
3. I mused 'Everyone in the world has their own story, own failure; so many people have experienced great suffering more than me.'
4. For families its beyond four letter alphabet 'Love,' love is conditioned with caste, religion, status, money, community and other extents.
5. A question that has remained in me about her is, "I have loved you", but you ask, "Have you loved me"?

The seventh vow was to rewrite the liner "Eppalodum Manam Solluvadu Sarialla" (Always never listen to your heart).

I eventually got married to Rekha, who taught me the right seven steps (vows) such as - blessing and prosperity, healthy married life, protect and increase wealth, share happiness and sadness, to take responsibility, be together, be truthful and trustworthy by being friends and bring harmony.

Prem Kahaan - Paanchavi Bhag

Love Status - It's Complicated

Love Status - It's Complicated

I hail from a village (Gopalpur) of Orissa, studied in a government school. I have seen life with poverty and struggle. According to 'Theory of Human Motivation' of Maslow's hierarchy of needs, my family and I were, in bottom (first level) 'Physiological Needs' such as "Roti, Kapda Aur Makan" nothing less than 1974 Bollywood movie on similar title and story line. According to Maslow's theory 'Love' in in the third level of hierarchy. As like any other aspirant, I moved to an engineering college in Bengaluru. This was the first time I spoke to a girl 'Nithya Nair', a beautiful girl with deergh kesh (long hair) and great smile. She reminded me of Naina (character played by Priety Zinta) of Kal Ho Naa Ho Bollywood movie. With my good performance in education and being gold medal winner in academics coupled with good job opportunity, 'Safety' second level of hierarchy and it looked easier. Inspite our daily conversations and belongingness/love, I am unable to convert this friendship into love.

This story is blended with a new twist 'Amrita Parhi' a school friend who is in love with me since school days. I was complete unaware of this, until and unless she expressed it few years ago. Amrita has unconditional love, she proposed me three times with a hope but she heard silence from me all the times. I am standing on a cross road - One direction Amrita has unconditional love, as she continues to love without even thinking about the kind of person I would have been in future; while we were at school. Her purity of love is immeasurable. Second direction is Nithya with whom I developed friendship and intimacy of belonging. Third direction is fourth level of Maslow's hierarchy 'Esteem,' parents and other family members have desires. I see there is a little hope from family to accept the third stage 'Love' and value it. I believe in this theory as each level is closely related to us. I now understand the relationship status option of Facebook 'It's Complicated.'

Adhuri Prem Kahaniya

Prem Kahaani - Chatha Bhag

Bachpan ka Pyaar - Sacha Pyaar

Intense Desire - Lust

History Repeats - Not to Repeat Again!

Bachpan ka Pyaar - Sacha Pyaar

March 2001, my father worked for police department and we moved to Giridih, Jharkhand State. Any newly admitted students were placed in section E. I was studying in high school, popularly known as 'Lambu' (Tallest) in the class. I had two close friends Jai Shankar and Amit Goswami and there was a girl on diagonally opposite bench 'Pallavi Puja.' She was a daughter of district judge - topper, beautiful and most admired amongst all. People bullied me often by calling 'Lambu' and this seemed intolerable to someone. Every relationship starts with some good note, it did happen to me as well. Unable to see I get bullied by others; Pallavi took charge and delivered an impressive speech. It brought silence in the class and seeing this soft corner by a topper to another topper from bottom of my class moistened my eyes. As a down to earth student, I thanked her for the support. I thank God for a typical Bollywood reply, 'I would have done this for anyone and you are special to me.' I also thank God, as she didn't bind this relationship as brother and sister. This incident brought us closer; she would often turn back and smile at me during lecture. Amit and Jai would act as catalyst in fostering this relationship.

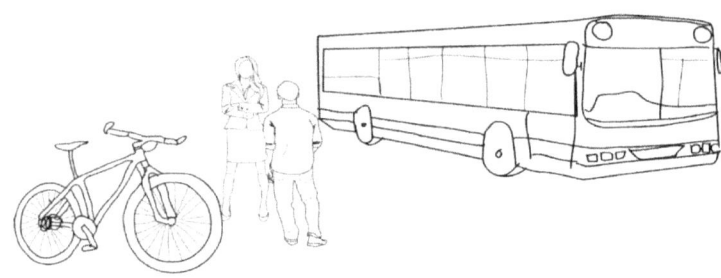

This all began stronger with 'Basket Ball' preparation. Basketball team members were preparing for the tournament at the school level. We used to be there since morning 5:00 am and practiced for long hours. Coincidental couple (that includes me) of us forgot to carry breakfast box. I walked into the class and requested if anyone could share breakfast with us during the break. Akash Rao gave his box before Pallavi would have given her box to me. Amit and Shankar saw her dismay and explained me later that, 'She apologized for not being able to give box before someone else; she was aware of your practice sessions.' She carried an extra box everyday to make sure that I need not have to starve. Only few can understand this complete belongingness.

It's good to get love in life; perhaps most craved among all the cravings! Sometime too much also brings agony. There was another girl Supreeta Suman seated on adjacent bench, perhaps had same feelings for me, like I had for Pallavi. My conversations with Supreeta irked Pallavi and this led to ugly or funnier scenes. To test Pallavi's love towards me, I cut my finger with blade; on hearing this from a friend - Pallavi came rushing, tears in her eyes and she hold the finger with her handkerchief. The scene was no less than Mohabbatein Bollywood movie Jimmy Shergill wounded hand is attended by Preeti Jhangiani. I, Amit and Shankar drove bicycle and she would use school bus to commute everyday. We used to follow the school bus until a point to bid goodbye for the day. She would turn and wave her hand from a window seat. We were seemingly the most perfect couple of all in the school. We celebrated most of festival or occasion together. I won "Best Class Representative" from all the sections of the year. I would always credit this small stepping success to Pallavi. There is belief or saying that, "All good things come to end" because there is a new thing to begin. I got news that Pallavi is moving away on 17th April 2002 from Giridih as her father got deputed to another town. I was not sure if we would meet again, on 14th April 2002 (at 11:30 am) I proposed her. She moved to another town that was 500 Km away, we had frequent conversations over phone. She underwent lot of stress as her parents, relatives and to a certain extent my parents weren't open for love as an institution. They felt that we are too young to be in relationship. It was 15th December 2002 that was the last time we spoke and we were inconsolable. In school we are taught there is only one 'God' and one religion 'Humanity,' but reality is something else. Did not our parents study from similar school of learning? People say this is not the age for love, does something like that exists? Till date I never got answer to such questions.

Intense Desire – Lust

Wikipedia defines, 'Lust as an intense desire or craving. It is a powerful psychological feeling producing intense wanting for an object, or circumstances fulfilling it.' My lust was 'personal inclination' trying to find Pallavi in others, whereas Parineeta lust was 'lasciviousness.' Parineeta joined our school, she was aware of my intense desire. She often would try to attract by her lascivious wink. This invitation some guys could have used or misused for the kind of lust it is. Knowing that I have joined Sanskrit tuition, she also joined. She would come half an hour early, as I used to arrive and wait in terrace thinking of Pallavi all the time. Parineeta used this opportunity at times and this was my first kiss. Inwardly I started feeling low about such frequent act by her. Two incidents called this off forever and I thank these incidents till date. My mother was away for two weeks, she was eager to visit my home. I was concerned of neighbours reactions and her thoughts of self-invitation. She barraged in no time after knowing over phone conversation about no one being at home. I would definitely admire the delicious food she cooked for lunch. Perhaps this is also a kind of lust. She laid her head on my shoulder and started to kiss. She started to undress herself; I pushed her and ran out of home for few minutes. I was nervous coupled with fast breath and tears in eyes, perhaps because Pallavi face was reminded. Parineeta felt this as an insult and she cut her wrist. She was hospitalized and most of them felt I was responsible. One of my friends asked me, 'Why am I punishing her?' I said to myself, live with her one-day and you will know the meaning of punishment. That day I understood that, each one of us have a different definition of love. Love being a universal thing. I would love the person, who respects life more than love. Things eased out and I moved to a new town in search of Pallavi.

History Repeats - Not to Repeat Again!

Feb 2005, a month away from X[th] standard board examinations, the preparatory examination scores weren't promising and it seemed to everyone that I would need another year to pass. There was a phone call that changed this view, Hi Lumbu, Kaisie Ho? (How are you?). It was nearly two and half year that I had heard Pallavi's voice. I was delighted; tears of happiness rolled and were surrounded with happiness of cloud. She insisted me to take admission for XIth standard at Ranchi. This motivation helped me to score 70 percent in X[th] standard board examination. Akash and I left to Ranchi to take admission in Ranchi to pursue science.

Although couldn't make into the same school of her but was delighted to see her and to be with her. She welcomed me with open arm and the pandorum vanished in no time. She helped me to find a house, my mother moved in and my family accepted her in no time. She did take lot of risk to meet me, as her parents disliked me because of their own perception. Being so young we used to talk about our marriage, children and their names. She would tell me always, 'Your name starts with my name ending Palla**vi.**' Only one thing I hid from her was about Parineeta. As I had moved on, didn't feel the necessity of past to be discussed. Every good element is associated with bad element; Deepash was in love with Pallavi. Akash, Deepash, Kaushal and others made a plot to break this relationship, as Deepash wanted to get her love. This story has all the element of a quintessential Bollywood potboiler. They used Parineeta story and built-up various barriers between us. Pallavi started avoiding me by taking Parineeta case seriously. All try to discuss/convince turned futile. On 27 Sep 2005 she called it off and pandorum revisited again!

Salman was a key friend in helping me to get back on toe with constant support, encouragement and reminding me about bigger picture of life. I met Anni (Aditya) during basketball tournament and he turned out to be a good friend. I was about to begin a new life, Anni narrated a story of girl who was in love in with a guy from Giridih, and the flash back was unbearable. As it involved Pallavi, me and with a twist of Shashank (Playboy), Shashank was as Pallavi's boy friend for 3 years in the past. This shook me off and I could never understand till date about Pallavi's attitude towards this hidden agenda. Till date I keep running away from falling in love with a fear of history might repeat. I have become weak, lost faith in the institution of love and doubt arises over every girl that I come across. People say that time is the best healer of pain but I feel that, "Time doesn't heal. We forget, bury, deny, mask or be immune to our past."

Adhuri Prem Kahaniya

Prem Kahaani: Satavam Bhag

Umbrella - Colors of Life

Umbrella - Colors of Life

Scoring 70% above in academics for a non-performer is one of the most delightful moments during education. I belong to this category for a while. There are many people like me those who hate 'Mathematics' subject and wish it didn't exist. Fear of this subject has made many students like me pursue or change course of studies. I did it by choosing diploma studies over science post tenth standard in the year 2004.

August 2004, I was on bicycle paddling towards my college, there was sudden drizzle followed by a heavy rain. I saw a girl with Kutai (umbrella) with jasmine flowers on her long hair. I parked my vehicle at a distance; couldn't take my eyes off her. I had only heard in movies or friends about 'Love at first sight,' I started experiencing that moment. I rushed in her Umbrella assuming a new colorful life would begin. I requested for a help to drop me till college, she was scared for a while, those heart beats still echoes me. Her soft hand still gives me feel of belonging. The walk so memorable that I forgot to pick bicycle from the road till a friend reminded me of it. I waited for her every day from 08:55 am till 09:00 am, those five-minute wait were perhaps longest waiting moments till date.

I finished first year in waiting and perhaps had very few unsaid meets. Patience and perseverance does pay off; unsaid moments turned to simple conversations during second year of diploma studies. These waiting's were painful at times; for instance I didn't get to see her for a week or seeing her speak to some other guy were like 'Jale pe namak chidakna' (Adding fuel to fire). Once it so happened that, I didn't get to see her for a week, this hope of waiting delayed to attend first hour class each day. According to Netwon's third law 'every action has equal and opposite reaction,' this was applicable on me as well, as I was canned by Head of Department and parents on such occasions. This act was an action and I used to show reactions to her. She gave me better reactions in her polite way; I was suffering from fever since a week. My heart would sink like 'Titanic' and feel sympathetic about the situation. With no further delay I proposed her without even trying to find out her reaction to it.

I didn't get any reply for next two days; on the third day she walked to me and left a notebook on my bicycle. I found only blank book with a peacock feather and a small paper rolled on the feather. This note read, 'I Love You Vishnu.' I wish there was some new law to explain the madness one would possess post proposal acceptance!

She turned out to be a good friend, mentor (helped me to clear mathematics subject in the consecutive years) and a lover. New colors were added to life and things looked promising. This inspiration made me take up an engineering seat; we set to achieve our distant dream. Unaware of colors could also fade with various physical or chemical impacts, it was 04:24 am I received a call from a friend. I neglected this call thinking it was a prank call from a friend of mine. In moments later, saw mobile beep with a new number - this was perhaps last call of Newton's third law. I heard cry and noise around; heartbeats became uncontrollable, fear surrounded by hearing 'Sharmila is no more macha.' A lorry hit Sharmila, while she was walking back from college on Jan 22, 2008. The colors faded in no time and life looks still till date! This pain only those can understand, the one who lost before having it.

Adhuri Prem Kahaniya

Prem Kahaani - Athavam Bhag

Diary, Maa Aur Nafrat

Rebel Star

Diary, Maa Aur Nafrat

Studying in a prestigious school is perhaps a proud factor; to this a girl bench mate would amplify this factor. I was bench-mate of Divya Dutta; we both had great admiration for each other. I had two close friends 'PG' (nickname though) and 'Shivkumar' they turned out to be my best friends till date. Change is universal phenomena, bored of being seated next to her, one day I decided to opt a seat next to Parag. People don't mind constant change but radical changes do catch a lot of attention, this happened to me as well. While being seated next to Parag, he was perplexed and he narrated a story of Divya being in love with me since 4th standard (6 years). There was Tsunami of emotions that took me back to my original bench mate. Divya had a personal diary and she would pen down day activities and I was one of the most important activities of the day! Although initially I felt it was intense but relatively shallow romantic attachment, in other words it was 'puppy love.'

Teacher taught us that, 'right to life and liberty' but it looked perfectly only in that period of learning. We were caught by a teacher, that teacher was a colleague of Divya's mother (she was also a teacher in the same school). Amanullah Ashraf saying is true, "To gain something, you have to lose something." There was drop in grading in many courses and it surfaced in no time. What else a teacher can do apart from grading lower? I wish I had known the full verse from Bible, "You shall love your neighbor... as yourself" (Mark 12:31), as I went to love bench mate more than myself. Every story is likely to have humiliation and I had my share of it quite earlier onwards. This grew as hatred towards most of the teachers and wait was worth. There is saying, "Every dog has its day," and I had mine too. I was chosen as a School Captain, this was the best opportunity to trouble teachers and students, as the power of a

Captain is higher than a teacher at times. Divya's mother might remember this throughout her life. Divya started seeing me a villain and she avoided at times (all times!). The story ended by completion of XII and may be 'Nafrat' departed us. The silent depart was though painful!

Rebel Star

Main Hoon Rebel Star

Some incidents in life make you weaker not stronger, there after I became rebellion by giving no soft corner to any girl. I had taken a seat in one of the top engineering college but decided to move to another college, as at times story doesn't end. I saw Divya in the same class of the chosen college. We had a group of 15 friends and Radha was one amongst them. She liked my rebellion behavior (will never knew what stuff girls fall for); we were just into second semester she proposed to me. I declined with aggression and she fell more for it. She did all that I was fond of in life. Before I could fall for her, "I was the king of kings, I had my own rules, rule for myself."

Things moved on and I fell in love all over again. Campus placements had begun and we were only two to be unplaced from the group. The sympathy shown by others is the worst situation. The liners such as, 'You will get a job, don't worry,' 'You deserve something better than this,' are more irritating than watching a 'Saawariya' movie 1st time or a bad movie. I decided to go for higher studies and a good GATE Rank secured a seat at Indian Institute of Science, Bengaluru. There was a last hope with a core company visiting campus placement and this time luck favored us. I wrote the aptitude test on her behalf. She cleared the further rounds and it was most joyous moment of her life. She wanted to give anything for this help, being emotional charged time - what else can happen? My family had accepted her and her sister knew about our relationship.

I joined for further education and she joined the organization. Her corporate world had begun, phone calls and meeting reduced over weeks. I would like to see the person that coined 'Corporate Life' and 'Personal Life' as I had only seen she is my life. She was busy at work or outing with team or friends most of the times.

Social media (Orkut those days) played a bigger role in relationship formation and relationship disillusions. According to The Wedding Report, out of 50 couples married in the U.S. in 2011, at least one met through social networking site. I often saw her photos uploaded with her colleagues and some looked too close. It may be true that people in relationships overanalyze their partner's online activity at social networks. We had constant arguments and quarrels; the relationship between us was getting fragile. I used to drive (1.5 hour) down to her office very often to just meet her for 15-20 minutes. Once I wanted to end all the analysis and rectify the issue. I waited outside her office for more than 2 hours and she was persuaded to come out of her office. I insisted her to sit on the bike and her colleague felt that I dragged her. She ran saying to her colleagues - 'I don't want this guy, go away.' This was first time I broke down!

Even if I want to live in peace, peace doesn't want to leave me. I saw a beep on phone, Hi, my name is Pradeep and I would like to talk to you. I was least interested to meet any unknown person. He urged me to meet as it involved Radha; one of the functions of adrenaline is to regulate heart rate, the rate was definitely higher for next few hours. He meets me over a coffee and revealed that Radha was his girl friend. He showed photographs of they being together, cannot explain this moment. He wanted me to help him to take revenge against Radha, as she had betrayed him and me. On the same day she had left to overseas for 3 months work from the organization. I left a message on her phone about it; she called as soon she landed asking me not to believe. According to Mikael Krogerus and Roman Tschappeler book on decision-making says that one need to have a strong gas pedal (over weak pedal) not to cheat others. She flew back in less than two weeks; I received this news from Pradeep. My friend and I went to her house to call off this relationship. There were heated arguments and her sister intervened to stop further mishaps. I always respected her sister, who was a sane. I told a final liner that, 'don't trust Radha, if she can cheat me then she might cheat you as well.' This depart was though painful but not silent, there was relief of taking away heavy burden. "A Love Needs Three Things - Pure Heart, Good Conscience, and Sincere faith." These three things have become precious to find now…

Prem Kahaani: Nauvam Bhag

Beautiful, Charisma - 40th lane

Intelligent - Secret Admirer

Emotional - 99.9 % Love

Practical - Contract Love

Adhuri Prem Kahaniya

Beautiful, Charisma - 40th lane

Some people have gifted 'Charisma' that can inspire devotion in others. I had mine own and four other people that came in my life in span of 10 years. It all started at 40th Cross, Tulip Road a lively road to remember. Perhaps the only lane in the entire layout that everyone were acquainted and even the new visitors weren't spared. I feel proud to say that I was the most handsome looking guy of that lane. As best of companies get to pick the best. I had a choice to pick my best in life too; I fell for the most beautiful girl 'Latha.' I say beautiful because other three had some other qualities but definitely not as beautiful as Latha. We had nearly six years of age difference. I was insecure at times as she was young and the movie 'What Women Want' had a strong impression on me. I agree trying to disagree about the cold hard truth; women in general are fickle minded specific to dating. I knew that I had charms to keep her receptive by teasing or admiring her and/or expressive about the care for her. However the charm I had, there was 'Surya Grahan' (Solar Eclipse) and others affected it. In no time I saw her with a new guy 'Harsh' he had a charm of 'doing Wheelie.' She fell for such act of Harsh and this proved me that she was just following her gut feeling and emotions to be with me for a while. The question you might have is, did I not try to get back my love? It seems obvious, Yes! But I believed that, 'You can't win back your love.' I learnt to respond to this by saying, 'Keep in touch.' This start made me realize -

1. Don't get to burn out all that has been made since the beginning of relationship
2. Be around with someone but not 'too much' around with the uncertain relationship
3. Prepare options by being in touch with previous girl friend so that one need not reek of desperation
4. Never love someone more than yourself

Intelligent - Secret Admirer

Some people are born intelligent understands life better than some others. I found one in my own house, a far relative studying in her XIth standard. We had created a nickname of each (I had to nick name of a girl named Chandini) so that we could never be caught. She had all the memories of childhood since age of seven as we grew up closely. To be frank I didn't remember most of them. I am saying that she was intelligent because, as a child she could have said at home that I smoke or reads adult books at my early age. She was a secret admirer. She fell for the kind of poetic lines I wrote in emails or letters that we exchanged. I never understood, why we still exchanged love letters inspite being in home? The risk of being caught was larger and separation was possible.

It was summer vacation and she was about to visit a camp of three weeks with her friends. I and along with a friends visited her camp to give her a surprise. I got introduced to her friends and we spent some time together. Next week was her birthday, to give another surprise I visited this time with a birthday cake. She looked relatively unhappy this time, I felt as she didn't feel like seeing me anymore? I had been there only for 2 hours but she spent more time with Rohit another guy from camp. Did she just simply forget about our date? I was low back home thinking about it. I decided to meet Rohit and express my love towards her. Rohit seemed a cool guy and he assured me that, there is nothing between them. I assume that there were some conversation between her and Rohit; she realized that I love her more than anyone else. She was matured to handle the situation made it look simple. Later she went to join a five years integrated course and things were swinging back and forth with similar such incidents. This happened till the last moment she got married to someone else. She was so open in discussion about the challenges we might face because of birth defects in a child born. I was thinking of love and she was thinking of biology aspects at times. The best part of this relationship was that it had discussions and mutual consents all the times.

Emotional - 99.9 % Love

One of the most crucial mistakes I did after breakup is rushing things. May be because, "The medicine for addiction of love is the love itself." You see, as emotions are blind because heart is irrational. We moved to a new place and this change was a welcome one! Our owners stayed above us and the love fell from the top floor. 'Varsha' some rains bring hope and makes everything better. I was weak at studies-graduated in subjects many a times, people had dejected me and last hope was to finish post graduation with a job to start. Varsha would remember all dates such as love anniversary; birthday's and she preferred celebrating all of them. I hardly remembered all these dates, not sure why such thing exists? It continues to cost under nose to many boy friends. I was unable to clear first few campus interviews and in middle of campus interview tensions she wanted few minutes to spend everyday. She had always the same question, don't you have 30 minute for your girl friend? My silence said it all; it turned out messy as days progressed. I felt that I never loved her 100%, as her expectations were nothing abnormal or away from my reach. Perhaps I should have stayed away for a while after a breakup. I still have nightmares about being departed from her at times.

Practical - Contract Love

I decided to have a friend around me rather than a girl friend. I received a call enquiry if the company hired on campus will also offer an internship. I had received an internship from the company that hired me on campus. This general enquiry turned out to become a contract love between Sheetal and me. In no time, I received a request at Facebook to add her as a friend. Neither I could see her profile photo nor any albums. I was curious to see her; she agreed to send a photo by email. I fell for her looks and wanted to meet her at the earliest. We spoke for a week before we met. I have never spoken so much till date with anyone in life as I did that day. We were emotionally charged and wanted to have a relationship. My mother was clear that I would marry someone in the same caste and unfortunately Sheetal belonged to some other caste. We set expectations that we would do all that we couldn't do in past relationship and depart after 2 years from now. That was the only timeline both of us had before we choose our respective life partners. By now I mastered the art of handling first date - I spoke about romance, past and about her. However the contract was, emotions do bring us back to ask: Can we give atleast try once by talking to our respective family members? This contract love had all the six seasons (Spring, Summer, Monsoon, Autum, Pre Winter and Winter) but season of love was not permitted.

Adhuri Prem Kahaniya

Prem Kahaani - Dasavam Bhag

Color Wheel Model of Love - Color, Color Which Color?

I agree to the theory of love developed by John Lee (1973). John Lee's compares primary styles of love are Eros, Ludos, and Storge to primary colors as red, blue, and yellow (don't correspond to specific colors). Let me take you through the complex journey of this color wheel model of love.

Passionate Love (Style Eros)

I was barely in my 9th standard and I fell for Sumiyya, this love can often be seen as romantic love in movies. I wore big Uncle Sam glasses all the time, looked no less than Agastya Rao (role played by Akshay Kumar) in Jaan-E-Maan Bollywood movie (Year 2006). The Eros love style according to this theory is said to be hopeless romantic, unrealistic and loving an ideal person. As this style focuses only on beauty, chemistry and at many times it's unrealistic and disappointing. Sumiyya ignored me as nobody, and even broke my heart by blowing me off by condemning me as a 'Bad Kisser,' compliment image of Emraan Hashmi.

Possessive Love (Style Eros + Ludos)

This theory holds well with my other love as well be it Suchitra, Apoorva, Sneha or any other in past. The scene is clear fantasy as I had a belief that, I was a hero and my girl friend was the heroine. This love style had a secondary love style mix of Eros and Ludos that could create mania or obsessive love this was seen while I was in love with Anjali. Anjali was a friend of my one of ex-girl friend. Inspite of knowing that she had a boy friend; I was a great contributor to break their relationship. This relationship saw a seesaw have Ludos (Casanova Kind) or more of Eros at times. It was like a roller-coaster ride at many times because of her jealousy and possessiveness of me being friends with other girls. She was first and last till date that I raised my hand on and I feel sorry about it. I was devastated finding her with another guy in an unexplainable scene.

Friendship Love (Style Storge)

Deepika was a sister of my ex-girl friend. She had a cruel, sadistic, drunk and abusive father, she and her family lived in fear if he was around or not. As I was still at fantasy world of being Hero and thought that I would get her out of the cell with sheer help. This began with friendship that eventually grew to be more intimate over phone before there was spurge of secrets - she was in love with Praveen. She wanted my help with this; I decided to refrain from act of this help. One fine day, I was with a group of friends and high on alcohol at a pub, whenever I am drunk, I preferred to stay at friends place. Two people in civil dress were in search of me and they reached the pub by tracing using network connection. My honest friends were also drunk and revealed my where about. The two people were cops and took me to station. I pretended not being able to recall and refused to accept knowing anyone by name Deepika. They opened a huge stack of paper that had SMS and phone call timings. Do I argue more? They asked me to narrate the whole story; her father found out that I was in his daughter's life. Finally she was traced with Praveen next day and I breathe a sigh of relief. Though my love may not be as passionate as Eros love, but it did last longer inspite the early refrain. All my heroism got over after this incident.

Selfless Love (Style Agape)

I always held love; out of hope...some day it will see light (Mai Pyaar Ki Ghanti Har Roza Raktha Tha. Ummid se...kabhi na kabhi Bajegi). Every break up gives something to each one of us; I received "Dum Maro Dum," always in company of fellow-hippies. The quote of W.C. Fields "When we have lost everything, including hope, life becomes a disgrace, and death a duty" seemed true until I understood the quote of Mason Cooley, "Every day begins with an act of courage and hope: getting out of bed." Anjana came into my life, a friend in past and hope seemed hopeful. I grew a selfless love towards her, life looked moving forward with hope. All looked perfect as we belonged to same religion, caste and creed. I wrote a love letter and gifted CD's of romantic movies. Her parents were in Middle East Countries and she often visited them. Her father found the love letter from her bag and handed it over to her mother. I am not sure what her mother advised her, she rang me up to call off the relationship. Is it Facebook status that changes anytime? 'Committed to Single?' That was actual first breakup in my all-short intense love stories. After three days she rang me to get back. I changed the status at Facebook again, 'Single to Committed.' Friends at Facebook are strange as they like and commented for both statuses. Things were getting back and she found my photo with my ex-girl friend in my mobile phone folder. This erupted to second break up; she could have asked me to delete it. I changed the status to 'Committed to Complicated.' This time status didn't have like but had questions, for which I didn't have answers. Had I knew the answer, the status wouldn't have been 'Complicated.'

I crawled though this patch and made her join MBA course. She was available only in the evening after her college hours and I was available only in the morning hours. I was doing my internship from 17:00 hours onwards. I had a transition state from Selfless love to Possessive love - I felt sick all over as she started partying with other guys. While I tried to restrict her from partying, she showed her transition from Possessive love to Logical love (Pragma). In logical love one looks for similar background, as she would question my social status most of time. I decide to choose Game-playing love (Ludus) to keep my lover from finding out about me. I started uploading photos taken with other girls at Facebook and tell her how happy I am. I saw that she got into Possessive love (Mania) transition state - for example she would advise me to hang out with only boys in Goa. May be we never had same color to last longer than those with opposing styles. We had fear in love but perfect love should drives out fear, as fear has to do with punishment. That's why all my love stories were never perfect.

Prem Kahaani - Gyarahavam Bhag

My Lady in the moonlight

My Lady in the moonlight

Movies are conventional in a sense specifically for falling in love, they might provide specialized ways to fall in love but don't educate in the practice of managing a relationship. They inspire people to fall in love but making people to pretend that is love out of people who have never understood the meaning of love. It is time that we learn to give proper attention to love. I say this because love is not just a feeling but it's also a known agreement. I admired the theory developed Psychologist Robert Sternberg's 'Triangular theory of love,' and I shall use 'Spirituality' to take this story forward. I shall use these partially to fit my story and with other examples.

I fell for a green-eyed girl with beautiful name apt for the eyes 'Lakshmi.' We first met at a college fest; her guardian accompanied her and I was with common school friends. I approached her to initiate a talk, although I agree that it was "love at first sight" something like infatuation love. She gave me a quick reply, *'my guardian is here!'* I was quick to bite back, would you be interested to talk if they weren't here? Smile and silence said it all. I received a call on the landline from her; it did take me by surprise. She went mad over me because of all the stupid things I did during college fest. Me being a silent listener gave me edge to make her fall for me. She wanted to be only friend and not to indulge into commitment or relationship. I understood that she has liking (intimacy) and I had infatuation (Passion). We would speak weekly once and I would turn the world upside down to attend the call. As this one call made up my week!

Along with infatuation, I grew liking or intimacy towards her, this is termed as Romantic love according to the above theory. We started to date; she often visited the locality I lived in. I used different telephone booth to talk to her, as there was always waiting queue for others to make distant calls in those days. During one of conversations over phone she revealed that, she likes one of the guy in my locality. I was taken by a blow and was curious to know the person name. The scene was no less than 'Beladingala Baale' Kannada movie, a challenge given by her to identify the person. The failure to identify frustrated me and she promised to reveal before the call is ended. I kept waiting for the call to end, but she insisted on continuing to talk. It was a great relief when the call ended after knowing that it was none other than me. I had to move to Hyderabad for higher studies because of some situation at home. I had moved to next stage of love known as 'Compassionate love' by deep affection and commitment. I dreamt about us begin together and return to native place was much awaited.

I was watching God TV and Pastor Benny Hinn during his ministries mentioned that the guy in green shelve less T-shirt be cautious on being in love. It reflected as if he was pointing towards me. In half an hour time I received a call from her and she proposed to me over the phone. I was taken aback from the message from Benny Hinn and asked her for sometime to reply.

This temptation is like Google and Facebook offering you a job and I need to pick one of those. I waited for this moment all these years and this temptation of loosing her otherwise; made me accept her proposal. I shall introduce you to bases (urbandictionary.com) that each relationship evolves with it. In the 'First Base' the couple kisses and there is often repetition to say Goodbye. It is believed to the beginning of being in love. We moved to next base in no time, termed as 'Second Base' in which the couples make out (up the shirt). I shall limit the readers' knowledge of understanding of 'Third Base' and 'Home run' and would let you guess. I had reached to consummate love, which is the complete form of love. I felt that we have become one flesh and accepted her as spouse. We had our nice moments of being jealous on each other, to quote one example - We (me and her) along with her friend (she) were walking on the road, I tripped her friend by accident and held her hip to get her back on foot. This created rift between them, friendship ka the end. I realized that day a liner *'A guy or girl is insecure about losing his girl or guy when he or she knows some else can treat her better.'*

We had major debates most of times it was about spiritualism, as I had my stance and strong belief. This debate was responsible to deteriorate stronger love into empty love. I did have the commitment, but the passion was slowly resting in peace. I am not sure, why people think Christianity as a religion?

There was silence of nearly three months on both sides. Love is like a sea surface that is subjected to waves. This becomes tall and unstable at times, no one would dare to touch as one can see violent destruction. Don't let your love sleep or you will grow poor. Never allow this sea to become stream of silence. Suresh another guy took advantage of this silence. I was unaware till the climax that she and Suresh had become intimate friends. I had only known earlier that they were friends.

Plot Maker

I shall introduce you now to Deepak (spoilt brat) a best friend for a while. Deepak had some issues with me (especially ego clashes for various reasons) and he was very much aware of every thing happening in my life. Deepak and Suresh devised a plot to get me into trouble. Deepak challenged me about me being having eligible driving license and being young blood decide to accept any challenge to prove that I can drive like Michael Schumacher. Deepak asked me to use his Alto to take a steep U turn and race straight on the road in the shortest possible time. Deepak was seated next to me; unfortunately I crashed the rear part of the car. There were all smiles on Deepak's face and he extends hand to ask money for the damage. I was shocked by his behavior, he dragged this issue to my parents and he used illicit words that shook me.

My parents gave patience listening to both of us. We decided to meet Deepak's guardian, Deepak's friends removed vehicle spark plug, unplugged the petrol wire of our parked vehicle while we were in talks with his guardian. My father assured to get it repaired and apologized on behalf of me. We found with the help of the house guard that Deepak's friend were responsible for our vehicle damage that was parked while ago. Father and I decided to talk to Deepak's guardian about it by requesting the guard to be witness.

The guard changed his statement in no time and this created a lot of misunderstanding between all of us. This is was perhaps first and last time I put my family into such a situation.

Deepak had become unbearable as he wanted his money for the damage rather it was intention to keep me troubled. He wanted to meet in a ground to settle the matter. I reached the empty ground and in sometime saw many common friends (15 in number) racing towards me. To my shock Suresh and Deepak arrived on the same bike and this took me a back.

Suresh narrated that he has an affair with Lakshmi; she had shared all those intimacy situations between her and you. He went to say, I am fine with it and accept her as she is. He suggested me to move away from her life. I can't explain this moment; I feel into the drainage and was numb for a while. He continued to prove that she was ready to elope with me (SMS was shown); people in her locality think I am her boy friend and guardian thinks that I was her boy friend. I couldn't forget his weird laugh that is highly nasalized for a very long time. I was in the utter shock stage and wanted to cry out. I was pulled out of drainage, Deepak asked me to give gold chain as a part of settlement otherwise he would reveal the intimacy bases that happened between me and her to my parents. All other 15 people (though my friends) were of opinion that I was reluctantly to pay for the damage. A friend of mine in the same locality saw me in middle of some trouble at distant place. He was famous / known for other reasons in the area (locality). Like a superstar he bashed each one of them and warned them to keep themselves away from me. I experienced the betrayal and loss of a close friend at the same time.

She wanted to get back after a while, I decided against it because of the following reasons -

1. She maintained steady relationship with Suresh and I was unaware of it.
2. I was convicted to God and would want my life partner also to be in future; this was misinterpreted as religion conversion.
3. She never accepted me as a life partner was a feeling generated finally.
4. After five years of being in relationship I realized that Benny Hinn was right.
5. I feel, "Love is good, but if it loses its loveless, how can you make it love again?

Prem Kahaani - Barahavam Bhag

A Love - Out of Balance

A Love - Out of Balance

People studying at institute like Indian Institute of Science, Bengaluru are perceived as geeks. There is often less spark of love amidst of serious calculations that take place in the air of the beautiful campus. With zest for business and will to manage the business choose MBA at IISc, Bengaluru. I although admire five models developed by Michael Jensen and William Meckling popular among MBA graduates known as "The Nature of Man." The first three that describes human behavior from perspectives of sociology, politics and psychology, fourth based on economics and the fifth one named as 'Resourceful, Evaluative, Maximizing Model," or REMM.

Meri REMM!

The fifth model describes my love story. Like any other bright young aspirant, bored with three years of full-time work and looking for a better position somewhere else, saw MBA as a launch pad. As I knew that a big salary, a dream job, signing bonus, recruiters queuing, the good life by pursuing MBA from a great place is always a best and safe bet. Like any other love stories, I happened to get a friend turned girl friend in the same class with its own moments. I always wanted to work and live in India, and continue to do so. According to this model, everyone is an evaluator. I had my own wants and she had her own wants, each of these wants comes only by tradeoffs and substitutions among them. These are expected to be there in any relationship as one's want may be money or car; while others want may be loyalty or integrity. The trouble with this want is its unlimited, each one of us want to maximize it.

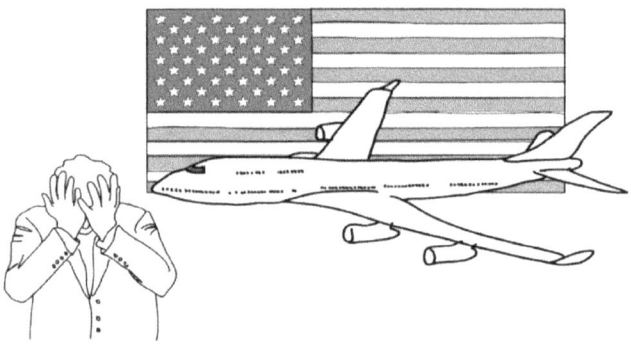

My want was to marry her, I proposed her to maximize it. Although because of differences in caste, parents were reluctant to agree. She had to leave to U.S. for onsite work, she returned exactly after one year to give breaking news of falling in love with someone else. I don't see shortage of news for the media to cover. The reason behind is, she was maximizing to be in U.S. and she found one at U.S. to trade off an Indian. I completely agree with Jensen and Meckling statement: "Like it or not, individuals are willing to sacrifice a little of almost anything we care to name, even reputation or morality, for sufficiently large quantity of other desired things." In other words pushed to the limit, everyone is a willing prostitute [Henry Mintzberg]. One thing is quite very well evident that everyone, everything has a price tag and REMMs exists everywhere. How true and sad is this?

Aaj Bhi Wapas Aane Ko Keh Do Mai Wapas Aajaounga,
Ye Pyaar Sirf Tere Liye Hai Wo Tere Saath Ache Se Nibha Paounga,
Duniya Chahe Kitni bhi Khilaf Ho,
Zindagi Tere Saath Nibhane Ka Faisla Kiya Tha
Aage Bhi Wahi Maanta Jaounga
– Ashar Neyaz

Inviting People to submit their *Adhuri Prem Kahaniya* to santosh.avvannavar@gmail.com for the next series of this book!

Sources

Mikael Krogerus and Roman Tschappeler, "The Change Book," Profile Books, 2012.

Jensen Michael C and Meckling William H, "The Nature of Man," Foundations of Organizational Strategy, Harvard University Press, 1998; Journal of Applied Corporate Finance, Vol. 7, No. 2, pp. 4-19, 1994.

Henry Mintzberg, "Managers Not MBAs," Readhowyouwant, 2009

Lee JA, *Colours of love: an exploration of the ways of loving*," Toronto: New Press, 1973.

Sternberg R J, 'A triangular theory of love,' Psycological Review, 93, 1986.

Sternberg R J, 'The Triangle of Love: Intimacy, Passion, Commitment, Basic Books, 1988.

Some images are extracted from www.Jumpstart.com

www.ingramcontent.com/pod-product-compliance
Lightning Source LLC
Chambersburg PA
CBHW070519130626
46555CB00003B/1287